I'M AFRAID YOUR TEDDY IS IN TROUBLE TODAY

To Sylvie
J. D.

For Isabel, Lillian, Geen, and Lantern
S. N.

Text copyright © 2017 by Jancee Dunn
Illustrations copyright © 2017 by Scott Nash

First edition 2017

Library of Congress Catalog Card Number pending
ISBN 978-0-7636-7537-0

17 18 19 20 21 22 LEO 10 9 8 7 6 5 4 3 2 1

Printed in Heshan, Guangdong, China

This book was typeset in Chowderhead.
The illustrations were created digitally and with love.

Candlewick Press
99 Dover Street
Somerville, Massachusetts 02144

visit us at www.candlewick.com

I'M AFRAID YOUR TEDDY IS IN TROUBLE TODAY

Jancee Dunn

illustrated by Scott Nash

CANDLEWICK PRESS

Oh, good. You're home. My name is Officer Hardy. I'm sorry to have to tell you this, but while you were out, we received a number of calls at the police station.

I'm afraid your teddy got in a little trouble today.

You'd better prepare yourself. It's not a pretty scene. As police officers, we thought we'd seen everything.

Well, we've never seen anything like this. As near as we can figure, the party started shortly after you left for school.

I still don't know how he did it, but your teddy bear managed to get hold of your phone. Apparently he called all your friends' stuffed animals and invited them over to your house.

As you can see, they took him up on his offer.

It appears they made pancakes—chocolate-chip pancakes. With blueberries. And rainbow sprinkles. And cherries. And whipped cream.

I regret to tell you that your bed is broken, too.

Twenty-five stuffed animals jumping on it at once will do that.

Then they took your crayons and—as you can see—drew all over the walls. (I must say, that penguin is a pretty good artist!)

We're still piecing together what happened after that, but we believe they moved to your mother's bedroom to play dress-up with her clothes. I'm sorry to report that the elephant may have been wearing pink frilly underwear on his head.

After that, they did, in fact, pour bubble bath
all over the floor for a sliding contest.
Not good. Not good.

From the hallway, we followed a sticky trail of paw prints to the living room. That was where they piled up your couch cushions and pillows into a kind of — I suppose the term would be "cushion mountain" — and used cookie sheets as sleds.

My partner and I have to admit, that was pretty clever.

After that, they decided to take a bath. Not an ordinary bath, I'm afraid. We don't know for sure who thought of the chocolate sauce, but we suspect it was the cow.

At around 2:15, your teddy bear and his friends had a dance party. How do we know? Because that's when the calls started coming in from your neighbors.

Oh, they were not happy. Not happy at all . . .

Finally, your teddy somehow managed to get one hundred balloons delivered to your place. The deliveryman is still outside, by the way, waiting to be paid.

I'm sure you understand all this has caused quite a commotion. When everybody scattered, officers went searching house to house, trying to catch all the guests. And some of them were pretty high up. We had to call in the fire department, too.

I suppose you're wondering where everyone is now.

Ta-da.

Sir, I take it you're the ringleader?
Come with me, please. I'm going to
have to take you down to the station.

You know . . .

I used to have a teddy bear once.
He looked a lot like you.

Gosh, I haven't thought about
him in years.

All right, this time I'm going to let you go—if you promise me that you're going to behave yourself from now on. I don't want to get another one of these complaints.

Come on, everybody. Let's get into the squad car and I'll drop you all off at home.

And, Teddy, I hope you're going right back into the house to help clean up. You be good, now.